BEAR IN SUNSHINE

Written by Stella Blackstone
Illustrated by Debbie Harter

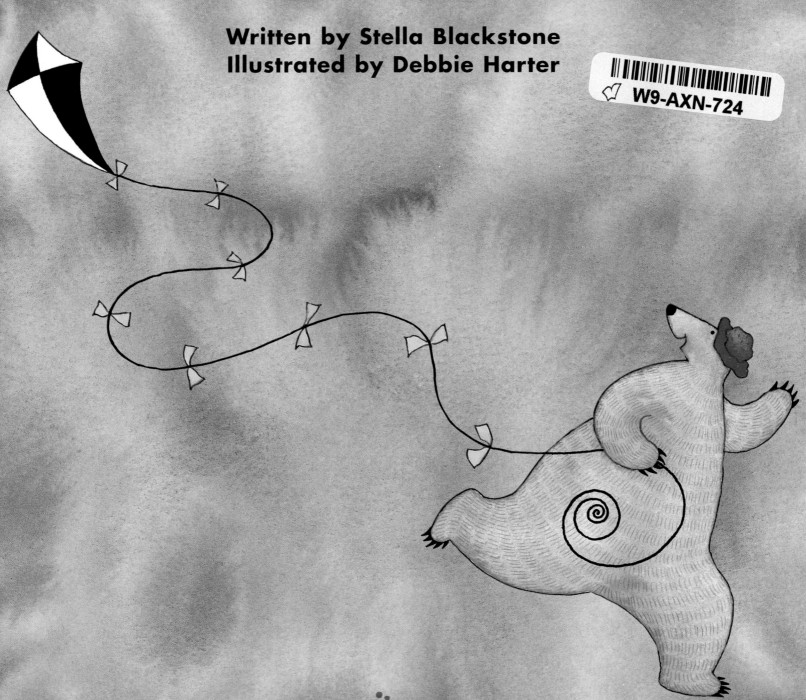

Barefoot Books
Celebrating Art and Story

**Bear likes to play
when the sun shines,**

Bear likes to sing in the rain.

He flies his red kite
when the wind blows,

When it's icy,
he skates in the lane.

Bear likes to paint
when it's misty,

When storms come,
he hides in his bed.

**When snow falls,
he likes to make snow-bears,**

When the moon shines
he stands on his head.

Whatever the weather,
come snow, rain or sun,

Bear always knows
how to have lots of fun!

Spring

Summer

Fall

Winter

For Felix – S.B.
For Julia and Isabella – D.H.

Barefoot Books
2067 Massachusetts Avenue
Cambridge MA 02140

This book was typeset in Futura
The illustrations were prepared in watercolor, pen and ink, and crayon on thick watercolor paper

Graphic design by Polka. Creation, England
Color separation by Grafiscan, Italy
Printed and bound in Singapore by Tien Wah Press Pte Ltd

This book has been printed on 100% acid-free paper

3 5 7 9 8 6 4 2

Library of Congress Cataloging-in-Publication Data

Blackstone, Stella.
  Bear in sunshine / written by Stella Blackstone ; illustrated by
Debbie Harter.
    p. cm.
Summary: Bear likes to play in all kinds of weather.
  ISBN 1-84148-700-7
  [1. Weather—Fiction. 2. Bears—Fiction. 3. Stories in rhyme.] I.
Harter, Debbie, ill. II. Title.
  PZ8.3.B5735 Be 2001
  [E]—dc21
                                                              00-012440